Valentine Poems

Valentine Poems

SELECTED BY
Myra Cohn Livingston

ILLUSTRATED BY
Patience Brewster

Holiday House / New York

TO DAVID McCORD

From: M.C.L.

From: P.B.
x o x

To: Marietta Brewster Gregg

MY HEART of HEARTS

Library of Congress Cataloging-in-Publication Data

Livingston, Myra Cohn.
  Poems for Valentine's Day.

  SUMMARY: A collection of twenty poems which celebrate
Valentine's Day.
  1. Saint Valentine's Day—Juvenile poetry.
2. Children's poetry, American. [1. Valentine's Day—
Poetry. 2. Poetry—Collections] I. Brewster,
Patience, ill. II. Title.
PS3562.I945P6 1987   811'.54   85-31723
ISBN 0-8234-0587-7

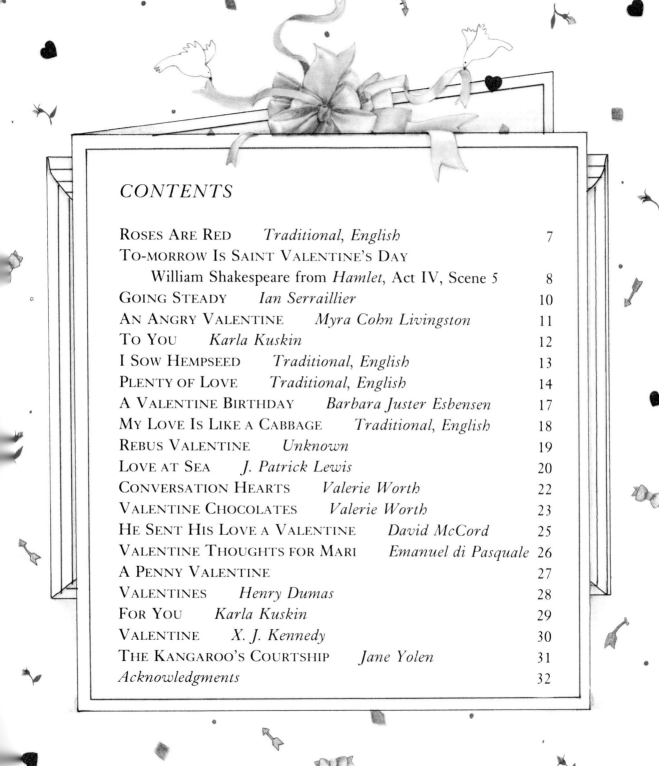

CONTENTS

ROSES ARE RED

Roses are red
Violets are blue
Carnations are sweet
And so are you.
And so are they
That send you this
And when we meet
We'll have a kiss.

Traditional, English

TO-MORROW IS SAINT VALENTINE'S DAY

To-morrow is Saint Valentine's day,
    All in the morning betime,
And I a maid at your window
    To be your Valentine.

WILLIAM SHAKESPEARE
from *Hamlet*, Act IV, Scene 5

9

GOING STEADY

Valentine, O Valentine,
I'll be your love and you'll be mine;
We'll care for each other, rain or fine,
And in ninety years we'll be ninety-nine.

IAN SERRAILLIER

AN ANGRY VALENTINE

If you won't be my Valentine
I'll *scream*, I'll *yell*, I'll *bite*!
I'll cry aloud, I'll start to whine
If you won't be my Valentine.
I'll frown and fret, I'll mope and pine,
And it will serve you right—
If you won't be my Valentine
I'll *scream*, I'll *yell*, I'll *bite*!

Myra Cohn Livingston

11

TO YOU

I think I could walk
through the simmering sand
if I held your hand.
I think I could swim
the skin shivering sea
if you would accompany me.
And run on ragged, windy heights,
climb rugged rocks
and walk on air.

I think I could do anything at all,
if you were there.

KARLA KUSKIN

12

I SOW HEMPSEED

I sow hempseed,
Hempseed I sow,
He that loves me best,
Come after me now.

Traditional, English

NOTE: *Repeated twelve times by a young woman circling a church in England to determine who would be her true valentine.*

PLENTY OF LOVE

Plenty of love,
    Tons of kisses,
Hope some day
    To be your Mrs.

Traditional, English

A VALENTINE BIRTHDAY
for Kai

Again today
we draw the heart around
your name   Our red crayons
bright with love—
the paper white as drifts
outside the door

Snowfall on your birthday!
Each
tumbling flake snipped
into lace   by the   scissoring
wind
Valentines! Valentines!
Valentines!

BARBARA JUSTER ESBENSEN

MY LOVE IS LIKE A CABBAGE

My love is like a cabbage
    Divided into two,
The leaves I give to others
    but the heart I give to you.

Traditional, English

REBUS VALENTINE

You may not [turnip] all for me
   The way I care for you.
You may [cantaloupe] your nose
   When I plead with you—
But if your [heart] should [beet] with mine
   Forever [lettuce] hope
There is no reason in the world
   Why we two [carrot] !

Unknown

19

LOVE AT SEA

February 14
Captain's Log
The Frisky Dog

Up through the fog came *The Frisky Dog*
    With me and my forty-man crew.
We were tightly packed, as a matter of fact,
    For *The Dog* is a bark canoe.
And the tides that ebb in the middle of Feb.
    Rolled in with a nasty howl,
But the crew stood fast to a two-foot mast——
    The flag was a paper towel.
Then the pop-eyed cook took a pop-eyed look,
    and he saw what we came to see:
The courtship swoon by a midnight moon
    Of an Octopus he and she.
They kissed on the lips and the slithery hips,
    They kissed on the suction cups.
And they bobbed in the brine like a ball of twine
    Till at last the bosun ups
And he shouts, "I'm Dutch, but I never saw such
    Sweet love on Valentine's Day!"
Then arm in arm . . . in arm . . . in arm . . . ,
    The Octopi swam away.

J. PATRICK LEWIS

CONVERSATION HEARTS

Such meek
Little tokens,
Sugary white,
Shy green, prim
Yellow and pink:

But spiced with
Mottoes: SURE
THING, OH BOY—
Each one like
A reckless wink.

VALERIE WORTH

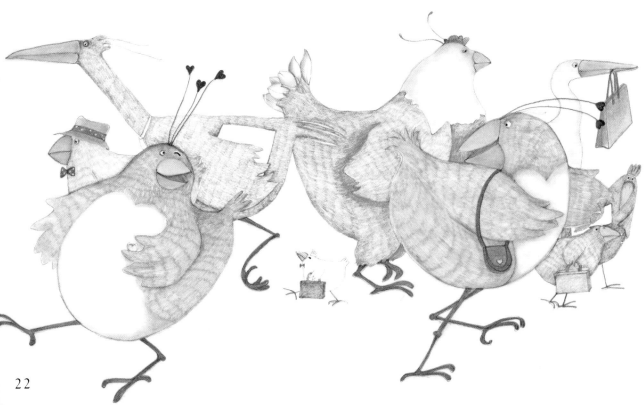

VALENTINE CHOCOLATES

Ordinary candy,
Perhaps—but
Boxed in a ruby
Heart, it grows
Exotic, mysterious;
Not to mention
The red cellophane
Wrapper, which,
Looked through,
Shows a marvelous
Scarlet world.

VALERIE WORTH

HE SENT HIS LOVE A VALENTINE

He sent his love a Valentine;
His love did not reply.
We never *dare* to care to sign
These things, I wonder why.

David McCord

VALENTINE THOUGHTS FOR MARI

I'd like to bunch your lips
into a goldfish pout,
let fly your chestnut hair,
smooth the strands out of your eyes,
stroke your sparrow hand
and say, "Let's go where
           the small brook frets.
           Let's join
           its silvery play."

EMANUEL DI PASQUALE

26

A PENNY VALENTINE

Silly, stupid, gawky elf,
Behold the portrait of yourself,
Dizzy, dozing, spiteful creature,
Mark each odious, hideous feature,
My heart shall never so incline
to choose *you* for a Valentine!

VALENTINES

Forgive me if I have not sent you
a valentine
but I thought you knew
that you already have my heart
Here take the space where my
heart goes
I give that to you too

HENRY DUMAS

28

FOR YOU

Here is a building
I have built for you.
The bricks are butter yellow.
Every window shines.
And at each an orange cat is curled,
lulled by the summer sun.
The door invites you in.
The mat is warm.
Inside there is a chair
so soft and blue
the pillows look like sky.
In all the world
no one but you
may sit in that cloud chair.
I'll sit near by.

KARLA KUSKIN

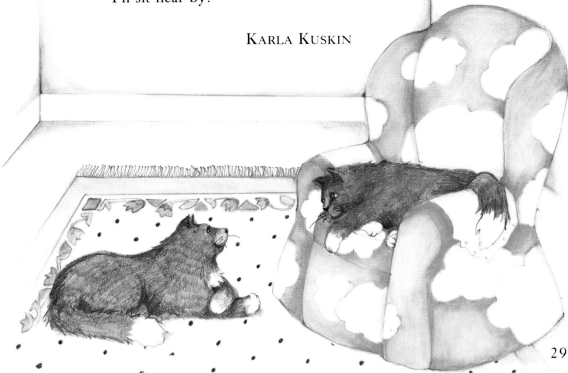

29

VALENTINE

If all the whole world's taxicabs
Came running to my call,
I'd park right by your door and honk
In the handsomest cab of all.

We'd drive to Spain, Maine, or Spokane!
Could anything be sweeter
Than ticking off a million miles
Upon a metal meter?

X. J. KENNEDY

THE KANGAROO'S COURTSHIP

"Oh will you be my wallaby?"
Asked Mr. Kangaroo.
"For we could find so very many
Jumping things to do.
I have a pocket two feet wide
And deep inside,
My dear, you'd ride—
Oh, come and be my bouncing bride,
My valentine, my side-by-side,
I am in love with you."

JANE YOLEN

ACKNOWLEDGMENTS

Grateful acknowledgment is made to the following poets, whose work was especially commissioned for this book:

Curtis Brown, Ltd. for "The Kangaroo's Courtship" by Jane Yolen. Copyright © 1987 by Jane Yolen. Reprinted by permission of Curtis Brown, Ltd.

Emanuel di Pasquale for "Valentine Thoughts for Mari." Copyright © 1987 by Emanuel di Pasquale.

Barbara Juster Esbensen for "A Valentine Birthday." Copyright © 1987 by Barbara Juster Esbensen.

Karla Kuskin for "To You" and "For You." Copyright © 1987 by Karla Kuskin.

J. Patrick Lewis for "Love at Sea." Copyright © 1987 by J. Patrick Lewis.

Myra Cohn Livingston for adaptation of "A Penny Valentine." Copyright © 1987 by Myra Cohn Livingston.

David McCord for "He Sent His Love a Valentine." Copyright © 1987 by David McCord.

Ian Serraillier for "Going Steady." Copyright © 1987 by Ian Serraillier.

Valerie Worth for "Conversation Hearts" and "Valentine Chocolates." Copyright © 1987 by Valerie Worth Bahlke.

Grateful acknowledgment is also made for the following reprints:

Atheneum Publishers, Inc. for "Valentine" from *The Forgetful Wishing Well* by X. J. Kennedy. Copyright © 1985 by X. J. Kennedy. (A Margaret K. McElderry Book). Reprinted with the permission of Atheneum Publishers, Inc.

Atheneum Publishers, Inc. for "An Angry Valentine" from *O Sliver of Liver* by Myra Cohn Livingston. Copyright © 1979 by Myra Cohn Livingston. (A Margaret K. McElderry Book). Reprinted with the permission of Atheneum Publishers, Inc.

Random House, Inc. for "Valentines" by Henry Dumas from *Play Ebony, Play Ivory*, edited by Eugene B. Redmond. Copyright © 1974 by Loretta Dumas. Reprinted by permission of Random House, Inc.